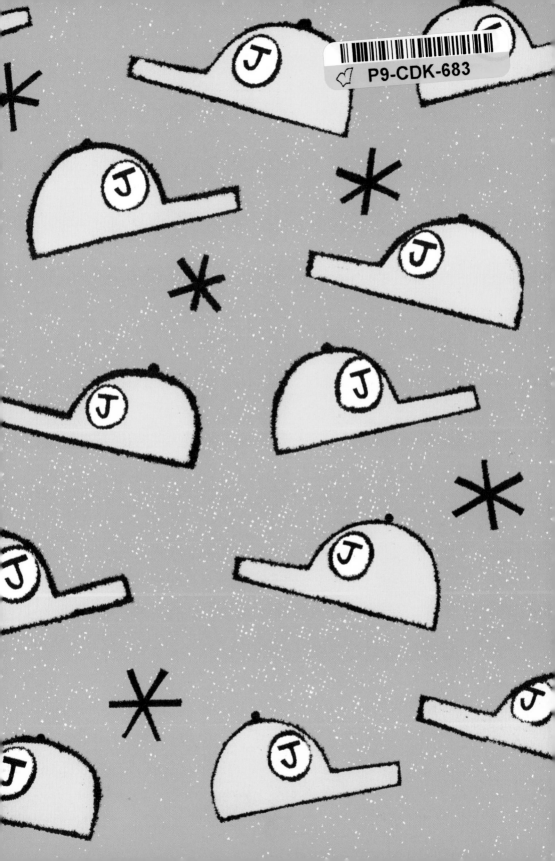

For Henry —MB

For Eleanor —GP

VIKING

An imprint of Penguin Random House LLC, New York

First published in the United States of America by Viking, an imprint of Penguin
Random House LLC, 2019

Visit us online at penguinrandomhouse.com

LIBRARY OF CONGRESS CATALOGING-IN-PUBLICATION DATA IS AVAILABLE.
ISBN 9780593113790

Manufactured in China
Book design by Greg Pizzoli and Jim Hoover   Set in Clarion MT Pro

10   9   8   7   6   5   4   3   2   1

HI, JACK!

Mac Barnett & Greg Pizzoli

Viking

1.

JACK

This is Jack.

Hi, Jack!

Look, Jack waves hi back!

Jack lives in a tree house.

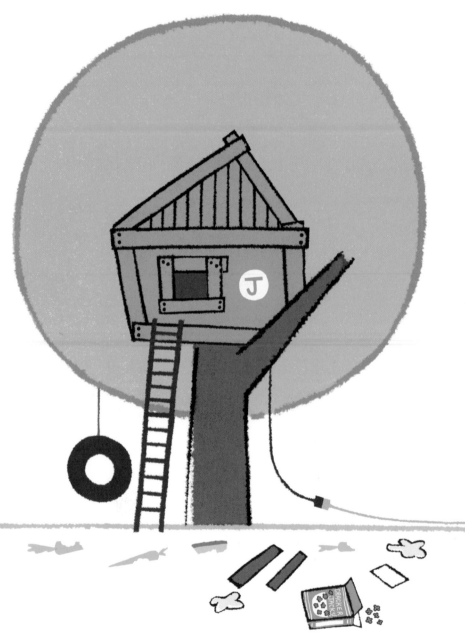

He loves to eat snacks.

How's that snack, Jack?

Look!

Jack comes down from
his tree to make a friend!

Bad Jack!
Jack, give that back!

Jack, give her bag back.

Give it back now, Jack.

Good Jack!

The Lady gives
Jack a pat.

That's a good Jack!

2.

REX

This is Rex.

Hi, Rex!

Rex lives on a farm.

Rex has white fur.

He likes to lick his fur.

That's a big lick, Rex!
A big, wet lick, Rex!

Rex has a black tail.
He likes to wag his tail.

Wag, Rex!
That's good, Rex.

Rex has red lips.

Rex! Why are your lips red?
Your lips are bright red!
Who did that to your lips?

Jack!

Bad Jack.

Jack, give it back.

Good Jack!

Back to Rex!
Look, Rex digs up
a bone.

Dig, Rex!

Jack, not the pink!

Stop that right now!
Stop, Jack! Stop it.

Give the pink
back too, Jack.

OK, Jack.

3.
THE LADY

This is the Lady.
Hi, Lady!

The Lady lives in
a big house on a hill.

Wow!
Her house is nice!

Here are her white walls.

Here is her nice art.

Here is Jack.

Jack!

Jack, why are you here?
Show us your hands.

OK, Jack.

Jack!

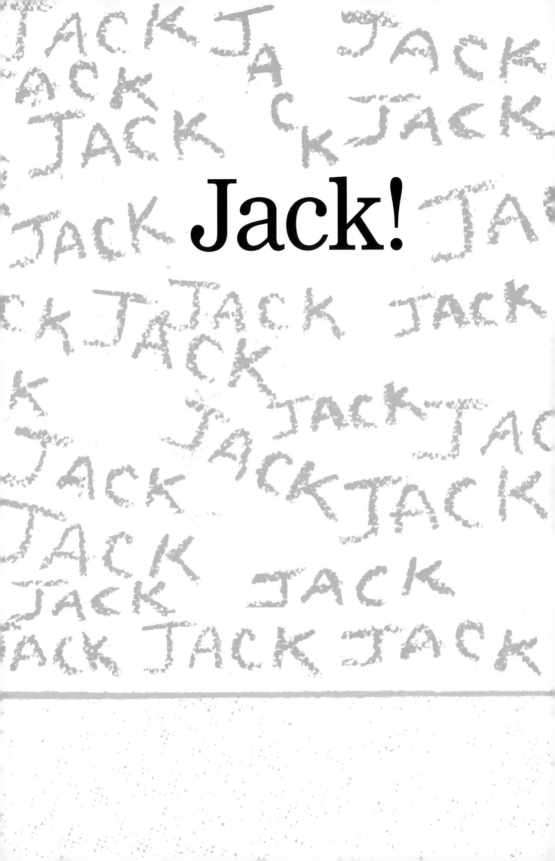

Jack!

Bad Jack!

Jack, you are bad.
You are a bad Jack.

A bad, bad Jack.

Oh, Jack.

Jack, don't do that.

Please cheer up, Jack.
Look, here is a gift!

What is it, Jack?

A snack!

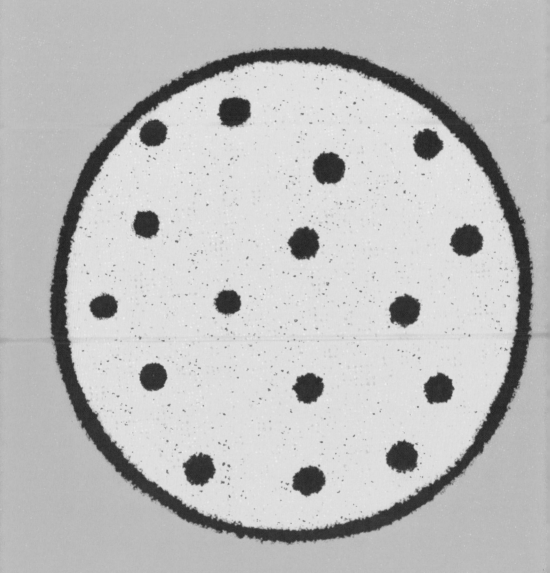

Jack loves snacks!

Jack, she gave you a snack.
What will you give back?

A kiss!

The Lady bends down
to get a kiss from Jack.

Ick!
Oh, Jack.

HOW TO DRAW...
JACK!

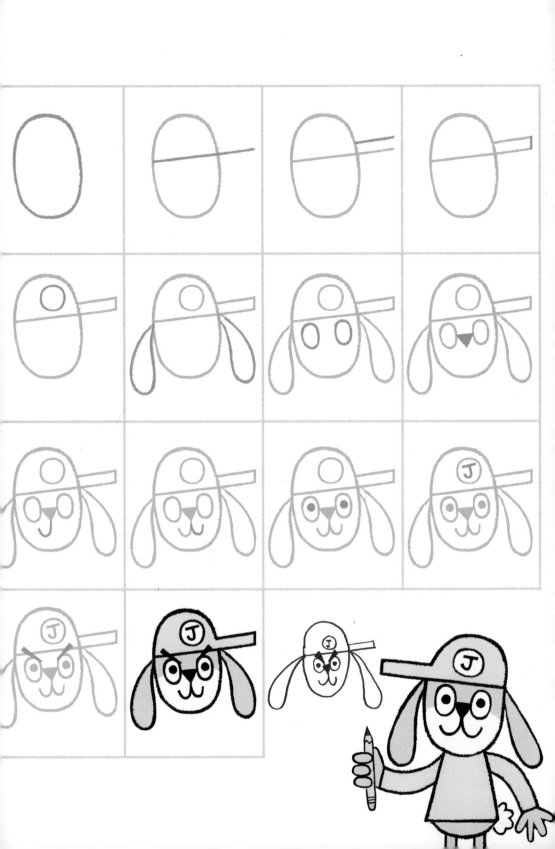

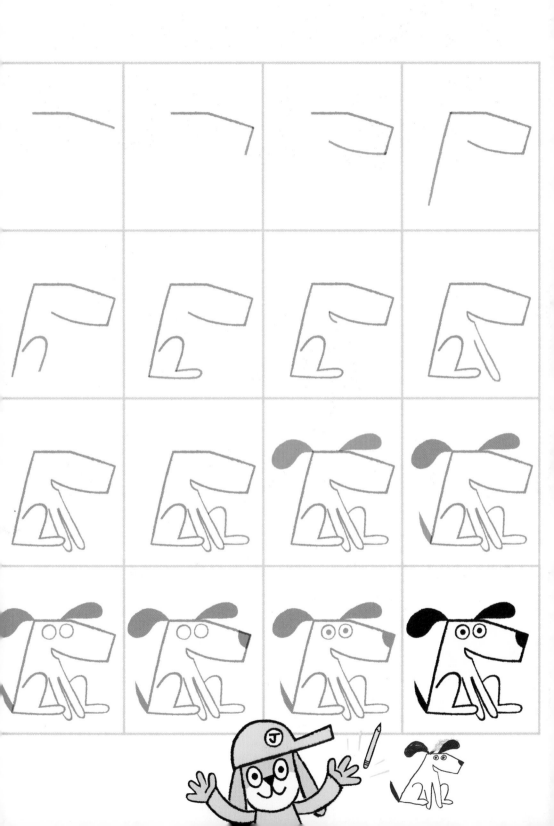

HOW TO DRAW...
THE LADY!

IF YOU WANT
MORE JACK, READ:

A JACK BOOK

JACK
BLASTS
OFF!

Mac Barnett & Greg Pizzoli